Jenny and the Cat Club

Favourite stories about Jenny Linsky

THE CAT CLUB
JENNY'S FIRST PARTY
WHEN JENNY LOST HER SCARF
JENNY'S ADOPTED BROTHERS
HOW THE BROTHERS
JOINED THE CAT CLUB

Written and illustrated by
ESTHER AVERILL

Young Lions

First published 1973 in the USA by Haper & Row, Publishers
First published in Great Britain by Young Lions 1976
Fourth impression May 1989

Young Lions is an imprint of
the Children's Division, part of
the Collins Publishing Group,
8 Grafton Street, London W1X 3LA

Printed and bound in Great Britain by
William Collins Sons & Co. Ltd, Glasgow

FROM THE AUTHOR

In this collection, you will find five of the earliest stories that I ever wrote about Jenny Linsky, the shy little black cat who lived in New York City. They were first published so long ago that children who used to read them in the beginning are now grown up and have children of their own. But readers continue to ask me the same question: 'Was Jenny real?'

Yes, Jenny was real — a very real cat. I knew her in the days when I lived in a house by the big garden where she lived with her master, Captain Tinker. Night after night, from my garden window, I watched little Jenny, wearing her red scarf, jump from a downstairs window of the Captain's house to attend the meetings of the Cat Club.

The Club would gather at the maple tree, which stood near a corner of the garden. The members came, not only from houses alongside the garden, but from beyond the garden's tall board fence. Indeed, this was a Club of neighbourhood cats and, as you might expect, they were of all sizes and descriptions. Each cat had his or her own personality.

The sight of so many different furry creatures sitting on the meeting ground beneath the maple tree aroused my curiosity. I longed to know more about them and their activities. It was not proper for me, of course, to intrude upon the privacy of Club meetings. But after a while, I began to discuss matters with Jenny's Captain Tinker, and he would tell me what he knew about his little black cat and the Cat Club. People elsewhere in the neighbourhood – kindly humans who loved all those cats – gave me valuable information, especially about events that sometimes took place beyond the garden fence.

Gradually, with a bit of assistance from my imagination, I was able to piece together these stories. I admit that in writing them I translated cat talk into language which humans could understand. I described cat happenings in terms that would be the most meaningful for you. However, I tried my best to keep the stories absolutely true to the personality of each cat and to the bright warm spirit of the Cat Club.

Esther Averill

THE CAT CLUB

OR
THE LIFE AND TIMES OF
JENNY LINSKY

In Captain Tinker's garden, once upon
a time, there was a Cat Club. All the
cats and kittens in the neighbourhood
were members. All but Jenny Linsky.

Jenny Linsky was a small black
orphan cat who lived with Captain

Tinker. He had found Jenny in the street where a dog was chasing her. No one knew where she had come from and the Captain took her home.

He was very kind to Jenny. She had cream and chicken every night for supper. Her coal black fur grew soft and glossy. Her yellow eyes began to have a happy look.

One day the Captain said to her, 'You and I must always be best friends.'

That made Jenny's heart beat fast.

But the Captain added gently, 'I think a little cat like you should go outside sometimes and play. Lots of nice cats live in this garden.'

Jenny had often heard the Cat Club singing after dark.

'They do have fun,' she thought.

But she was too shy to say 'hello' to them.

'Shy little cats need help,' thought Captain Tinker to himself.

Captain Tinker, who was an old sailor, liked to make things and many years ago had learned to knit. He knitted a woollen scarf for Jenny – a bright red woollen scarf to go with her black fur and yellow eyes.

How Jenny loved that scarf! How brave she felt when she was wearing it! And one fine night she put it on and

8

went into the garden.

It was a lovely garden full of flowers and trees and bushes. On three sides were rows of pink brick houses. On the other side was a tall board fence that kept the dogs away. Jenny and the Captain lived in the brick house that was covered with ivy.

Jenny crept softly through the grass and found a hiding place beneath a rosebush. There she waited for the Cat Club. She waited a long time.

Suddenly a slim white cat sped

through the grass, dashed up the maple tree and began to sing. This was Concertina, the Club Secretary. She sang:

> *Come all ye cats and kittens*
> *With your whiskers and your mittens*
> *Come a-running, come a-running*
> *To the Cat Club Jamboree.*

Mr President came first.

Mr President was a well-fed cat who always wore a collar with his name and number on a tag. He walked slowly out of his brick house and took his place – the 'Chair', he called it – on the meeting ground beneath the maple tree.

Then the others came. They came one by one and two by two from darkened doorways and over the tall board fence. They formed a circle in front of Mr President.

CONCERTINA, IN THE MAPLE TREE, GIVES THE SIGNAL
FOR THE CATS TO COME

Just before the meeting, MR PRESIDENT speaks to his young nephew,
JUNIOR. The fluffy cat is BUTTERFLY. The twins are ROMULUS and REMUS.
The cat jumping over a flower is MACARONI. SOLOMON, the wise cat who
can read, sits on his books and watches the two great fighters, SINBAD
and THE DUKE. The two cats in earnest conversation are the
sweethearts, ARABELLA and ANTONIO.

11

Mr President opened the meeting and spoke a few brief words about a money matter. Afterwards the Club moved to the porch of Concertina's house.

Jenny stretched her neck and peeping through the rose leaves saw everything that happened.

The spotted twin cats, Romulus and Remus, crawled through the kitchen window and returned with a large paper package.

'A feast! A fish!' cried all the cats.

They tore off the paper and devoured the fish.

After they had licked their paws and whiskers, the lovely Persian cat, Butterfly, brought out her nose flute and began to play. The cats sang and danced and joked until the wee small hours when, one by one, the Club went home.

The last cat to go was Jenny Linsky. She had not dreamed that cats could have such fun.

Night after night she crept into the garden and watched the Cat Club from behind the rosebush.

'What clever cats they are!' sighed Jenny. 'All of them can do things. Look at Butterfly. She plays a nose flute. Look at Macaroni. He can dance on his hind legs. And what can I do?'

Poor little Jenny! There was nothing she could do. But she was content to watch the others at their fun and frolic.

One night, to her surprise, Romulus and Remus who were going to the meeting, poked their noses right into the rosebush and cried gaily, 'Hi there, sister, you're the new cat, aren't you?'

The twins were in such lively spirits that Jenny did not feel afraid.

'Yes,' she answered, 'I am Jenny Linsky.'

'Well, Jenny, wouldn't you like to join the Cat Club?' asked the twins.

They did not give her time to answer.

They whisked her off between them.

But when they reached the meeting ground, fear overcame her. All the other cats were there, staring at her with their gleaming eyes, as if to say, 'And what can you do, little black cat? WHAT CAN YOU DO?'

This was too much for Jenny. She gave a yowl of terror and fled home.

Next morning Romulus and Remus went to Jenny's house, looked through the garden window and called, 'Jenny! Jenny Linsky!'

Jenny did not answer. She was lying on a soapbox in the cellar.

The twins had come to cheer her up and they went away, discouraged.

In the afternoon the Persian cat, the lovely one named Butterfly, pressed her silky face against the windowpane and called, 'Jenny! Jenny Linsky!'

Jenny Linsky did not answer. She was still lying on the soapbox in the cellar.

Butterfly, too, went off, discouraged.

In the evening the entire Cat Club, singing loudly, trooped through the

garden on their way to Jenny's house.

Mr President came first.

Behind him walked Butterfly, playing on her nose flute.

Concertina followed. She had a high soprano voice and led the singing, and behind her, one by one or two by two, the singers marched.

First came Romulus and Remus.

18

Next, Mr President's young nephew, Junior, accompanied by Solomon, the bookish cat.

The fancy dancer, Macaroni, followed. He was waltzing.

Behind Macaroni came the sweethearts, Arabella and Antonio.

Lastly marched the two great fighters, Sinbad and the Duke.

All of them were singing:

Meow and a purr! We want HER!
Jenny! Jenny! Jenny!

Alas! They sang too loudly.

A man who could not sleep threw down a bucketful of water and broke up their fine parade. The members scampered home to dry their dripping fur.

They did not meet again until the following night when they had other plans and did not go to Jenny's house. It was summer and in the summer Cat Clubs are very busy.

So in the end the Club in Captain Tinker's garden quite forgot poor Jenny Linsky. Still, you cannot blame them. You cannot expect other cats to think always of your troubles.

Jenny, who was ashamed of having run away, now stayed indoors. Time dragged. Now and then she played games with Captain Tinker. But when night came and she heard the cats in the garden, she longed to be with them.

'And that will never happen,' she sighed. 'They are too clever. All of them can do things. What can I do? Nothing.'

Time passed.

The birds flew south. The honeysuckle and the rosebush lost their leaves.

Winter came and everything was frozen. Then Captain Tinker flooded the garden and made a pond where the boys and girls could skate.

One day while Jenny watched the skating from the window, she turned suddenly to Captain Tinker.

'I should love to skate,' she said. 'That's something I *could* do.'

Jenny was surprised that Captain Tinker did not answer. She went to him and put her paw upon his arm.

'Captain,' she said, 'if I could only have some skates.'

Captain Tinker remained silent. He sat in his armchair, puffing at his pipe and looking thoughtful. Jenny did not know that out of the corner of his eye the Captain watched her as she climbed the stairs.

Upstairs she hunted for skates in the chest of drawers and on the cupboard shelves. She found nothing.

In the night while Captain Tinker was asleep, Jenny came downstairs and searched the downstairs cupboards.

She ransacked the drawer where Captain Tinker kept his fishing tackle.

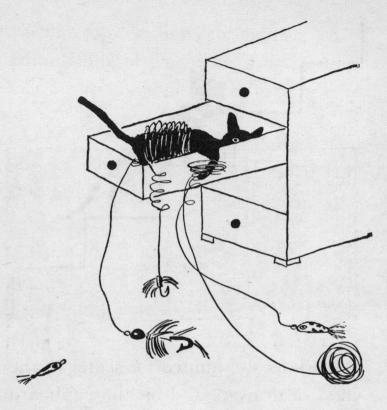

She found hooks and lines and corks —
but no skates.

In November it snowed — the first
snow storm Jenny had ever seen. All
afternoon she watched the snowflakes
falling.

By evening the garden was entirely white. Jenny stole outside and hunted in the drifts. She found snowflakes

shaped like flowers and stars and spiderwebs – but no skates.

'I'm glad Jenny has gone outside at last,' thought Captain Tinker. 'Now we shall see what we shall see.'

Bright and early the following day the Captain went to his workshop in the cellar. He closed the door behind him and would not let Jenny in. All morning she could hear him tapping with his hammer.

The mysterious hammering and tapping went on for many days. On Christmas Eve Captain Tinker came upstairs with something in his pocket. Jenny watched him as he lit the Christmas candle and pulled back the curtain.

'The stars are out,' said Captain Tinker, looking at the sky.

As he said it, he took out of his pocket four little —

Could they be real?

Jenny stared.

She reached out and touched them – oh, so gently – with her paw. They were real, and they were silver, and they had sharp shiny blades.

'Ice skates!' she whispered. 'Silver ice skates! Oh, Captain . . .'

The Captain strapped the skates on Jenny's paws. They fitted exactly. Her ankles wobbled for a moment; then she felt quite steady. Captain Tinker tied her scarf and she went into the garden.

At the pond she hesitated.

'Which paw goes first?' she wondered.

She struck forward on her right front paw and glided. Then with her left hind paw she gave a shove and glided farther. She began to skim across the ice.

It was a pretty sight to see her skating with her red muffler streaming,

and her bright skates flashing in the moonlight. She cut figure eights and

flowers and stars.

The Cat Club saw her. They were at the other end of the pond and had been singing Christmas carols. Their mouths hung open and their bulging eyes were fixed on Jenny Linsky.

No one in the Club had ever seen a cat skate.

Suddenly Romulus and Remus cried, 'Jenny! Jenny Linsky!'

And all the other cats cried, 'Jenny! Jenny Linsky!'

She glided towards them.

Romulus and Remus dashed to meet her and before she knew it she was standing in front of Mr President.

'Mr President,' said Romulus and Remus, 'we hope that this black cat, a friend of ours, will now be asked to join the Club.'

Mr President looked at Jenny with his beady eyes.

'What is your name?' he asked.
'Jenny Linsky,' she replied.
'Where do you live?'
'In Captain Tinker's house.'
'Can you do anything?' asked Mr President.

'I can skate,' said Jenny proudly.

'Yippetty-yip-yip-yip!' cried all the cats.

When the cheering died down, Mr President addressed the Club, saying, 'The question is, shall our distinguished guest, Miss Jenny Linsky, who can skate, be asked to join the Cat Club. All cats in favour raise a right front paw.'

Every member raised a right front paw.

'All cats opposed kick a left hind leg.'

No one kicked a left hind leg.

Two cats went into the bushes to count the votes. They came back quickly and whispered in Mr President's ear. Mr President looked satisfied.

He turned to Jenny.

'Miss Jenny Linsky,' said Mr

MR PRESIDENT
(his newest picture)

CAT CLUB EMBLEM
This emblem will be made in
little medals for the members
to wear on their chests

President, 'the votes have been counted.
I have the noble honour to inform you
that you are a member of the Cat
Club.'

'Mr President,' said Jenny in a high
clear voice, 'and you, my trusty friends,
I thank you.'

Jenny could have made a longer
speech. But the Cat Club crowded
around her, hoping for a chance to
touch the silver skates.

CONCERTINA

ROMULUS

REMUS

JUNIOR

ARABELLA

ANTONIO

BUTTERFLY

THE DUKE

MACARONI

SINBAD

SOLOMON

J. LINSKY

JENNY'S
FIRST
PARTY

One summer night the little black cat, Jenny Linsky, climbed over the tall board fence at the end of the garden behind her home, crept through a private passage and came out on South Street.

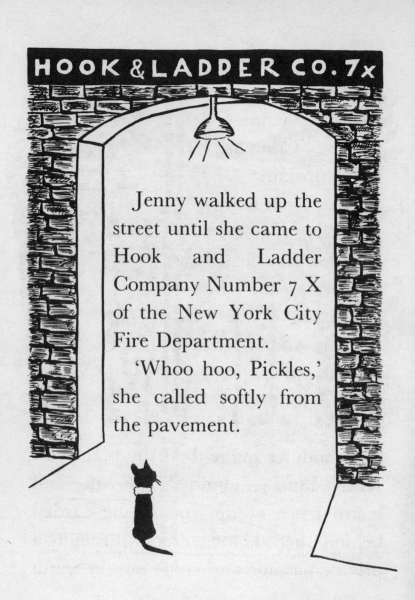

HOOK & LADDER CO. 7x

Jenny walked up the street until she came to Hook and Ladder Company Number 7 X of the New York City Fire Department.

'Whoo hoo, Pickles,' she called softly from the pavement.

Pickles, the big, spotted, yellow cat who was the mascot of the Company, was upstairs ... playing draughts with the firemen.

When he heard the 'whoo hoo', he put on his fireman's helmet, slid down the firemen's pole, walked around the Hook and Ladder for good luck and went out to Jenny.

'Hi, Jenny,' said Pickles. 'What's doing? Where's Captain Tinker?'

Pickles was referring to Jenny's friend and master, the old sea captain, Captain Tinker, in whose house she lived.

'Captain Tinker has gone out,' said Jenny. 'He went out for supper.'

'What about the Cat Club?' Pickles asked, referring to the Club that met each night in Captain Tinker's garden.

'Something happened,' Jenny said. 'Mr President has told us that we can't meet again until it gets straightened out.'

'So you came here,' said Pickles, with a note of kindness in his queer, rough voice. 'So you came here to see your old friend, Pickles.'

'Yes, Pickles, I was lonely,' Jenny said.

Then she added shyly, 'Pickles, let's go somewhere. Let's have some fun.'

'I haven't any money for a party,' Pickles said. 'I'm broke. Have you any money?'

'No,' said Jenny, 'I'm broke, too.'

Jenny poked her paw in a crack in the pavement, as if she hoped to find a penny.

When no coin appeared, she said, 'Captain Tinker says that money isn't everything.'

'I'm not so sure,' said Pickles.

He turned his big, spotted, yellow, face towards the sky to find out about the weather. The night was crystal clear. Up high the moon was swimming like a great liquid silver dollar. As for the stars, Pickles felt that he could touch them if he held out his paw.

'All right,' he said to Jenny. 'Let's get going. You lead the way.'

'*Me* lead?' gulped Jenny.

She was just a small black cat and very shy. She had never been a leader.

'Tell me where you want to go,' said Pickles briskly.

'Let's go and get Florio,' said Jenny.

Florio lived around the corner. He was a young, golden-haired cat who was as handsome as a prince. Best of all, he was gentle in his ways and very gay.

Florio was lying upstairs on a satin cushion when he heard their soft 'whoo hoos'. He stood up, pulled back the window curtain and gave a silent signal.

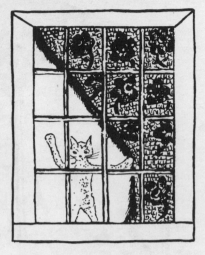

A few minutes later Florio came out. He had had to wait and slip out secretly. His mistress would have died of fright if she had known that he was on the pavements of New York.

When Florio realized that Pickles was wearing his fireman's helmet and that Jenny had on the red scarf that her master, Captain Tinker, had knitted, he borrowed an Indian feathered

43

headdress from the doorman.

'Hello,' said Florio, as he joined his two friends on the pavement. 'Are we going to have a party?'

'Not unless you have some money,' Pickles answered.

'I haven't any money,' said the golden-haired cat. 'I'm broke.'

Pickles sighed.

But Jenny said, 'It would be fun to have some fun.'

Florio looked at Jenny.

'Where would you like to go?' he asked.

'Oh, anywhere,' said Jenny.

Pickles said to her, 'Name one idea.'

Jenny thought a moment. She tried to think what her master, Captain Tinker, would do in such a situation.

'Certainly he would do s-o-m-e-t-h-i-n-g,' Jenny told herself. 'He would think up games or have a catnip hunt or *something*.'

A bright idea flashed through her mind.

'Let's find a doorway and a secret passage!' she cried. 'It might lead to an enchanted palace!'

'And to hidden treasure!' Pickles cried.

'And Indians!' cried Florio.

They started down the street: Jenny with her bright red scarf, Pickles with his fireman's helmet and Florio with his Indian feathered headdress.

They walked on many streets. But all the streets were lighted with electric lights. And all the doors were locked.

After a while, Pickles was ready to go home. Even Florio was growing discouraged. But Jenny was having a wonderful time. She had never been on the streets at night.

'Oh, please,' she begged, 'let's go just a little farther.'

So they went a little farther, choosing streets that were darker and more filled with mystery and moonlight.

All of a sudden Jenny said, 'Do you hear what I hear?'

They listened.

They looked down a small side street that had no light but the moonlight. Over the rooftops rose the laughter of many cats.

'It sounds like a party,' said Pickles.

And he straightened his fireman's helmet.

Florio straightened his Indian feathered headdress and said, 'Yes, perhaps we'll have a party after all.'

But the little black cat, Jenny Linsky, did not say anything. She was too excited. She had never been to a party.

After a moment Pickles said, 'You two wait here. I'll go and scout.'

Pickles disappeared down the dark

street, came back shortly and said, 'I've found the gate.'

Then he led his two friends to a wooden gate that was open just wide enough to let a cat slip through. One by one they did slip through and in the moonlight, in a big, deserted yard, they saw what they were looking for: a party, a party just for cats.

There were striped cats and yellow cats and white and grey and speckled cats. All of them were dancing in the silver moonlight.

How their legs flashed! How their whiskers glittered!

In the centre of the party was a fluffy cat who danced the tumba rumba.

'That fluffy one must be Alice Featherlegs,' whispered Florio to Pickles.

Pickles whispered, 'You're right. It *is* Alice.'

Alice Featherlegs!

Jenny had never seen her before. But she had heard of Alice. What cat had not heard of Alice Featherlegs, who was famous for her beauty and the way she danced the tumba rumba?

Before long Alice Featherlegs caught sight of the three new arrivals. She ran over to them, and her soft fur made a rustling sound as she drew near.

How elegant and full of grace she seemed! Jenny could not take her eyes away from her.

But Alice did not even glance at Jenny. Alice looked only at Florio and Pickles. She acted just as if she never spoke to little cats.

Alice's behaviour made poor Jenny

feel extremely small and plain.

Jenny could hear the fluffy creature say to the two bigger cats, 'How wonderful of you to come! I think we may have met before. But anyway, will you join our party?'

'We should like to very much,' said Pickles, bowing like a fireman.

Then Pickles said, 'Miss Featherlegs,

may I present our friend, Jenny Linsky?'

Alice answered in a far-off voice, 'My, what a pretty little cat. But isn't she too young to dance the tumba rumba?'

Jenny wanted to say, 'I don't know how to dance it. But I think I could learn.'

Try as she would, Jenny could not make the words come out. And before she knew what had happened, she was sitting on the top of an upturned basket.

'This is just the place for Jenny,' Alice said to Pickles and Florio. 'She can watch us dance, or she can take a nap.'

Take a nap! What a horrid thing to say to a little black cat at her first party.

Jenny sat absolutely still and held

back her tears.

Florio, whose light paws tingled with the music, said to Jenny, 'Please don't worry. We'll only dance once.'

And Pickles said to her, 'That's true. Then we'll come right back to you.'

Jenny watched her two best friends go off with Alice Featherlegs. Immediately they were the centre of the party. Time was nothing to them. Time is nothing to a cat when he is dancing.

Pickles and Florio danced on and on. Now and then they glanced at Jenny to make sure that she was safe. They could see her sitting safely on the basket, but they could not see that she was lonely.

Jenny had never felt so sad in all her life. She began to wish that she were at home with her dear master, Captain Tinker. She wished that she were sitting on the Captain's lap.

The Captain knew how to comfort her. He always told her that her troubles could be straightened out.

Right now it seemed that she could almost hear the Captain's voice. It seemed to her that he was saying, 'Jenny dear, don't sit there, feeling sorry for yourself. Get up and do something. Get up and dance.'

'I don't know how to dance the tumba rumba,' answered Jenny.

Anc the Captain said, 'Then dance the dance I taught you.'

The Captain meant the old-time sailor's dance: the sailor's hornpipe.

Although Jenny had danced the sailor's hornpipe once or twice at home, she had never danced it in public. So she climbed down to practise it behind the basket. She wanted to make sure that she knew all the steps before she danced it in front of Alice Featherlegs.

Jenny stood up on her left hind leg and twirled around. She waved her left front paw above her head and softly gave the sailor's cry: 'Hi ho!'

Then she skipped gracefully and twirled around on her right leg. And once again she called, 'Hi ho! Hi ho!'

'That's the way to dance the hornpipe,' Jenny thought.

She was surprised to find that she could dance it very well, and she went on practising it behind the basket, out of sight.

When Pickles happened to look over to make sure that Jenny was all right, Jenny was nowhere to be seen. All that could be seen was one black front paw appearing from behind the basket and then disappearing. In a second another front paw rose and flapped and disappeared.

Pickles was terrified.

'Jenny is drowning!' he cried.

He left Alice Featherlegs and rushed off to rescue Jenny. Florio ran after him. But when they looked behind the basket, there was no water. Jenny was not drowning. Jenny was on dry ground – dancing the sailor's hornpipe!

'Well, well,' said Pickles with a note of admiration in his queer, rough voice.

And Florio cried, 'Oh Jenny, will you dance with me?'

Pickles wanted to dance with Jenny, too. So Jenny said she would dance with both together, and they led her out into the moonlit yard.

How proud she was to teach them how to dance the sailor's hornpipe!

The three friends were soon dancing
so beautifully that all the other cats
rushed over to them. All but Alice.

Alice was left alone in the middle of the yard.

After a while she grew tired of being by herself. She joined the others, and several of her old friends taught her how to dance the sailor's hornpipe. But she could not dance it half so well as Jenny.

Jenny led the dancers. Oh, what fun they had! Their cries – 'Hi ho! Hi ho!' – rose high above the rooftops and drifted towards the moon.

Jenny danced until the early hours of the morning. Then her small black paws grew weary.

Pickles said to Florio, 'It's time to go.'

The three cats thanked the others for the lovely party.

Florio said to them, 'We'll have to have another party soon.'

And Jenny said, 'I'll give the party at my house. All of you must come.'

'Hi ho! We'll come!' cried all the cats.

All but Alice Featherlegs.

Jenny looked at Alice.

'Alice, you must come, too,' said Jenny. 'My master, Captain Tinker, will be nice to you.'

Jenny, Florio and Pickles pattered down the street towards home. At Jenny's house they sighed happily and parted.

Jenny crawled through the window

that her master, Captain Tinker, had left open for her. She went upstairs and sleepily rattled the doorknob of the Captain's bedroom door. The Captain heard her and got out of bed and let her into the room.

He took her in his arms and stroked her gently and untied her bright red scarf.

'Oh, Captain, we went dancing,' Jenny murmured, 'and I could dance for ever!'

The Captain looked at her and smiled.

Jenny had fallen asleep.

WHEN
JENNY LOST
HER SCARF

O, happy
Are we
On our
Annual Spree.
—FROM AN OLD
MARCHING SONG
OF THE CAT CLUB

One fine spring day the little black cat,
Jenny Linsky, sat at the open window
of her house. Dreamily she watched her
red scarf drying on a clothesline in the
garden.

'I'm glad the housekeeper washed
my scarf,' thought Jenny. 'Now it will
be fresh and clean for me to wear to the
Annual Spring Picnic of the Cat Club.'

But all at once a rough dog, whom
the club had christened 'Rob the
Robber', rushed out of a cellar,

grabbed Jenny's scarf and ran off with it. It happened so quickly that Jenny didn't have time to think or be scared. All she wanted was to get her scarf away from Rob. So she cut through the garden, climbed over the tall board fence and ran down the alley into South Street.

By sniffing the pavement, Jenny found the trail of the dog and the scarf. She followed the trail as far as the Toy and Catnip Shop which stood at the corner of the street.

Here Rob's trail turned sharply around the corner, into Mulligan Street.

'I guess he's taken my scarf to the Den of the Dogs,' thought Jenny with a shiver.

She crept close to the Toy and Catnip Shop and peered cautiously down Mulligan Street towards the dark cellar where Rob and his band of dogs had their den. There was not a dog in sight.

'They're probably all inside, pawing my scarf,' thought Jenny. 'But I'll go into the den and get my scarf, even if they chew me up.'

Fortunately, at this very moment, two friendly voices called out, behind her, 'Jenny! Jenny Linsky! Wait for us!'

Jenny turned and saw the twin cats, Romulus and Remus, standing on the kerb across the street. Of course she waited for them, and when the traffic

light turned from red to green, the patchy-coated twins came bounding over to her.

'Jenny, what has happened?' cried the twins together. 'What are you doing out in the street, without your scarf?'

'That Rob the Robber stole it,' replied Jenny indignantly. And she told them what had happened.

The twins said, 'Well, Jenny, we admire your spirit, but really you're no match for Rob. Why don't you go home? We'll try to get your scarf and bring it to the Cat Club tonight.'

The twins pushed Jenny with their speckled noses. She ran home and waited.

She waited all that afternoon; waited until the sun dropped in the west; waited until night descended and the cats began to gather beneath the maple tree that stood in the far corner of the Captain's garden. When they had formed a circle in front of their President, Jenny crept over to them.

Romulus and Remus had saved a place for her between them, and as she squeezed into it they whispered to her, 'No luck. No luck.'

'Silence, please,' ordered the President. 'The meeting is about to open.'

'But this is important, Mr President,' the twins objected. 'It's about Jenny's scarf. It was stolen this morning.'

Mr President quickly opened the meeting.

'Jenny,' he said gravely, 'will you please step forward and tell us what happened?'

Shyly the little black cat stepped into the circle in front of Mr President.

Jenny's neck felt cold and bare without her red wool scarf tied snugly around it. And all those pairs of cat eyes staring at her through the moonlight frightened her. But she knew she had to speak. She must make the Cat Club understand how important was the

scarf she had lost.

'Mr President,' said Jenny, 'this morning Rob the Robber stole the red wool scarf my master, Captain Tinker, knitted for me to wear wherever I go. Captain Tinker has gone off to sea on business. When he comes home, I don't want to have to tell him that I lost my scarf. I'll try my best to get it back.'

'Thank you, Jenny. You may be seated,' said Mr President. 'Romulus and Remus, kindly tell us what you know about this robbery.'

As Jenny sat down, the twins stepped forward and explained how they had met Jenny and why they had sent her home.

'Then we followed Rob's trail to the Den of the Dogs on Mulligan Street,'

said the twins. 'But Rob was guarding
the door. He shouted to us that Jenny's
scarf was hanging on a nail in the den,
and that a thousand cats could never
get it back because the den would be
guarded day and night.'

'Thank you, Romulus and Remus,'
said Mr President. 'You may be seated,
for I can see that Madame Butterfly
wishes to speak.'

As the twins returned to their seats,

the Club's most beautiful member, the silvery Madame Butterfly, stepped forward.

'This robbery bristles my whiskers,' she declared. 'At noon, while I was out shopping, I met Romulus and Remus. They told me all about it. Of course, I feel that what happened to Jenny this morning happened because of what happened here last Hallowe'en.'

'Excuse me, Madame Butterfly,' interrupted tough Sinbad. 'What has what happened here last Hallowe'en got to do with our Annual Spring Picnic? Tonight the Club's supposed to talk about our picnic plans.'

'Patience, Sinbad,' replied Butterfly. 'I have a surprise for all of you. Look!'

Slowly Butterfly opened her silvery right front paw. Between two of its velvety pads lay a diamond, brighter than a star. Jenny's yellow eyes almost popped out of her head, and cries of *Oh!* and *Ah!* and *Please may I touch it?* went round the Club.

Butterfly, guarding the diamond, said, 'I have removed this jewel from the trimming on my nose flute, and I'm giving it to the Club to pay for whatever it costs to get back Jenny's scarf. What's left over shall be spent on buying food for our picnic.'

79

 Sinbad asked, 'Do you mean we can't have our picnic until we've found Jenny's scarf?'

'Exactly so,' replied Butterfly. 'Last Hallowe'en Jenny risked her life to bring me my flute, which I had lost. To do this, she had to outsmart Rob and all his dogs. Today Rob got even with Jenny by stealing her scarf. But I intend to help her get it back with this diamond.'

Mr President took the diamond happily, for there was not a penny in the treasury.

'Mr President,' cried Sinbad, 'why not buy Jenny a new scarf, instead of waiting to get the old one back? Then we could hold our picnic on Saturday night, as we'd planned.'

The members nodded. And Butterfly said, 'Jenny, shall you and I go to the Toy and Catnip Shop and try to buy a little scarf?'

'No,' thought Jenny to herself. 'All the diamonds in this city couldn't buy me anything as nice as my old red scarf. That was the first scarf I ever had.'

But Sinbad was saying, 'I know where we can buy fine fishes for a picnic – cheap.'

'Oh!' sighed Jenny. 'The Club *does* want the picnic. Without the picnic, it won't seem to them like spring at all.'

She raised her voice. 'Thank you, Madame Butterfly. I'll go shopping with you.'

So Butterfly took back the diamond and arranged to call for Jenny at ten o'clock next morning. And from break-

fast until ten, Jenny polished her fur
and whiskers for the shopping trip.

'Jenny, how nice you look!' said
Butterfly, when she arrived. 'Come,
let's start before those dogs get wind of
our plans.'

Side by side, the two cats crossed the
garden, jumped over the fence, passed
into South Street and dashed to the Toy
and Catnip Shop. As they pushed open
the door, the owner looked at them
with surprise.

'My good woman,' said Butterfly,
'have you a red scarf for my young
friend to wear?'

The woman did not seem to understand.

'Maybe a pink scarf,' suggested
Butterfly.

Again the owner failed to understand.

'Or a little blue scarf,' said Butterfly, flashing the diamond she carried in her paw.

'Oh!' exclaimed the woman. 'If you want to buy a toy for her, she might enjoy this duck.' And she placed a big toy duck on the floor in front of Jenny.

'A duck to play with, when I need a scarf,' thought Jenny miserably. But to be polite, she gave its tail a push.

'Quack!' shrieked the duck. 'Quack! Quack!'

'Come, Jenny,' said Butterfly in disgust. 'If this store doesn't understand us, no store will. We might as well go home.'

That night, at the Club, Butterfly had to report that the shopping trip had failed. As she returned the diamond to Mr President, she said, 'There's nothing left to do but think of a way to get the old scarf back.'

'Yes,' agreed Mr President, 'let us close our eyes and think.'

So they all closed their eyes and thought, but no one could think of a plan. When the meeting finally broke up, everyone felt blue. Saturday night was drawing near, and it looked as if there wouldn't be a picnic.

As Jenny paused in the window of her house, on her way to bed, she murmured, 'The Club has done everything it can to help. If we're to have the picnic, I must get help from somewhere else. But from whom?'

Suddenly she remembered her friend, the Fire Cat, Pickles, who worked in the Fire Station in South Street. Pickles had once told her, 'If you ever need me, let me know.'

Jenny knew it wouldn't be much fun to travel on the streets at night, without her scarf to bring good luck. Perhaps those dogs would catch her. Never mind. She'd do the best she could. And without thinking of her own safety, she ran to the fence, jumped over it and sped down South Street towards the Fire Station. Fortunately she reached it safely and found Pickles on duty.

'Jenny, what's the matter?' he asked.

'Rob the Robber stole my scarf,' explained Jenny. 'And he's hung it in the Den of the Dogs. The den is guarded so no cats can get in. And one thing has led to another. Now our Club can't have its Annual Spring Picnic until we get back my scarf.'

'I wish I could help you,' said Pickles.

'Pickles,' said Jenny, 'you're a friend of the Fire Dog, Buster. He's a good dog, and maybe you could ask him to tell Rob to give me back my scarf.'

'Buster's a very good dog,' agreed Pickles. 'But he works in a fire station the other side of town. I won't see him until the Firemen's Ball in the summer. You run home, Jenny. It's long past your bedtime. I won't forget what you've told me. With dogs like those Mulligan ruffians, anything might happen.'

It happened that same night, while Jenny was asleep in her basket in her upstairs bedroom, next to the street. She had been dreaming that the Club was holding the picnic, and she was with them, eating a delicious fish, when she was awakened by the fire engines roaring along South Street.

Sleepily she thought of Pickles on the front seat of the hook and ladder –

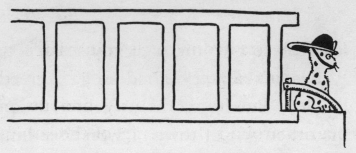

riding to put out the fire. How safe she felt because of Pickles! How proud she was to know him! She was drifting back to sleep when she heard a *psst! psst!* beneath her window.

Jenny ran to the window and peered into the street. On the pavement stood Romulus and Remus.

'The Den of the Dogs is on fire!' cried the twins. 'Those dogs were playing with a box of matches they stole this afternoon. Jimminy whiskers! What a fire they started! We're going back to watch the blaze.'

The twins dashed away and disappeared around the corner of the street.

'I must go, too,' thought Jenny. 'My red scarf is in the den. There's no time to lose. I'll take the short cut through the garden.'

Jenny hurried down the stairs that led to the garden window. As her black paws sped from stair to stair, her mind kept saying, 'My red scarf is in the den, and Pickles has gone over there to fight the fire. Pickles can save my scarf, but he'll be too busy to think of it himself. When I get there, I'll remind him.'

Jenny leaped through the open window and ran across the garden to the fence. There she gathered her little black legs together and made ready to jump to the top of the fence. But when she tried to jump, her hind legs seemed to stick to the ground.

She tried again, and again her hind legs stuck to the ground.

She tried a third time, and for the third time something seemed to hold her back.

'It's just as if I weren't meant to go to the fire,' she thought. 'But why shouldn't I go?'

Suddenly the reason became as clear to her as the moonlight on the grass. Pickles' duty was to fight the fire and keep it from spreading.

'I mustn't bother Pickles,' Jenny decided. 'I mustn't ask him to stop his noble work in order to rescue my scarf. I mustn't even go and watch the fire, because if Pickles saw me he might remember my scarf and try to save it, when he shouldn't.'

Jenny glanced around the garden. It was utterly deserted.

'I expect all the Club has gone to the fire,' she thought. 'And I expect my scarf will soon be burned to ashes. No scarf means no Annual Spring Picnic. Oh! How the Club will hate me!'

Jenny longed to run home, crawl into her basket and hide her little black face.

'But that would be cowardly,' she concluded. 'I'll wait here at the fence. I'll wait and wait until someone from the Club comes home by way of the fence and will tell me the news. Maybe Madame Butterfly will come, and I could beg her please not to think about a scarf for me, but to give all the diamond to the picnic.'

At last Jenny could hear the hook and ladder returning slowly down South Street. The bell of the hook and ladder was ringing, 'Fire's out! Fire's out!' And after a while she heard four paws turn into the alley.

'That's no one from the Club,' she thought. 'I know the sound of all their paws.'

Pit-pat! Pit-pat! The sound drew nearer and nearer. It was like the fire bell, saying *'Fire's out! Fire's out!'*

Jenny heard someone jump, and saw a huge spotted yellow paw clutch the top of the fence. Above the paw rose a shiny black helmet and a yellow face. Then came the left front paw, clutching something red.

'Catch!' boomed the Fire Cat.

Jenny reached up and caught the

scarf. It hadn't been burned at all!

'Oh, thank you, Pickles! Thanks a thousand million times. Was anybody hurt?'

'Nobody hurt,' replied Pickles. 'But the den is flooded with water from the hose. I think those dogs have learned a lesson.'

'Pickles,' said Jenny shyly, 'with all you had to do, how did you remember my scarf?'

The Fire Cat laughed.

'At first I didn't have time to think of anything but helping the firemen squirt the hose,' he said. 'Then the Chief told me to rest. So I stopped and looked at the crowd. All the Cat Club was there – all but you.'

'What did you think when you didn't see me?' asked Jenny.

'I thought of your scarf,' answered Pickles.

'Oh, Pickles! I wish I could have helped you rescue it!' cried Jenny.

'You helped me best by staying home,' said Pickles. 'It takes courage for a little cat to wait patiently and unselfishly at home when her best red scarf is in a fire.'

The Fire Cat raised his yellow paw, touched his helmet and saluted Jenny.

At that same moment, something moved towards her through the bushes. When she turned, Mr President was standing on the moonlit grass, with all the members of the Cat Club.

'Jenny,' began Mr President, 'our Club is proud to see you honoured by the Fire Department for your patience and unselfishness.'

'Aye! Aye!' sang the members.

'We of the Cat Club also wish to honour you,' said Mr President. 'We wish to honour you for this reason. Although you're small and shy, you always do the best you can.'

Jenny's heart felt warm and happy.

'Jenny,' continued Mr President, 'our Club shall hold its Annual Spring Picnic on Saturday night in Washington Park, three streets north of our garden. You, Jenny Linsky, wearing your red scarf, shall lead us as we march through the Arch of Victory that guards the entrance into the picnic grounds.'

JENNY'S
ADOPTED
BROTHERS

The little black cat, Jenny Linsky,
sat down beside the rosebush in her
master's garden. The roses were in
bloom, the birds were singing and the
sun shone brightly.

'How lucky I am to have this garden
and a master like the Captain,' thought
Jenny. 'I wish every cat could have the
nice things I have.'

At that moment Jenny was surprised

to see a black and white cat sitting alone in a corner of the garden.

'There's a cat I've never seen before,' continued Jenny. 'He looks as if he wanted something. He's bigger than me, but maybe I can help him.'

Jenny straightened the red scarf she was wearing, and ran over to the stranger.

'Hello,' she said. 'My name is Jenny Linsky. What's yours?'

The stranger removed a red ball he was holding in his mouth, and said, 'My name is Chequers.'

'Chequers what?' asked Jenny.

'I can't remember my last name,' said Chequers. 'So much has happened that I've forgotten lots of things.'

'Chequers is a very pretty name,' said Jenny in a comforting voice. 'And it's a good name for you,' she added as she examined the furry, black checks on his thin, white legs. 'But you look hungry. Don't they feed you at home?'

'I haven't any home,' said Chequers.

'No home?' cried Jenny. 'Oh, it isn't fair! Why, Chequers, I have this lovely garden and that brick house with the ivy on it. And my master, Captain Tinker, is the nicest master in the world.'

As she gazed at Chequers' darling, heart-shaped face, she had a bright idea.

'Chequers,' she said, 'I'm Captain Tinker's only cat. If you'll come home with me, I'll ask the Captain to adopt you.'

'Thank you,' cried Chequers joyfully. 'I'll go with you as soon as Edward comes.'

'Edward? Who is he?' asked Jenny.

'Edward is my big brother,' replied Chequers. 'His last name is Brandywine. We met when both of us lost our homes, and we've been brothers ever since. Where I go, Edward goes too.'

'Chequers,' sighed Jenny, 'maybe my master isn't rich enough to adopt two —'

Jenny didn't have time to finish her sentence. Edward had heard his name, and he came hurrying out of the bushes.

He was a tiger cat with a broad, white chest and beautiful eyes. But in those eyes there was the sad look of cats who have no homes.

'Edward,' said Chequers, 'this is Jenny Linsky. She's going to ask her master, Captain Tinker, to adopt us.'

Just then a bell rang in the garden.

'That's the Captain calling me to lunch,' explained Jenny.

Chequers picked up his red ball and started towards the Captain's house.

But Jenny said, 'Wait. It isn't easy to get *two* cats adopted. We must work out a plan.'

She thought hard for a moment and

then said, 'I have it. I'll try to get you adopted one at a time.'

'Jenny,' begged Edward, 'please try to get Chequers adopted first. He's smaller than me, and very hungry. I'll wait outside your house until you call me. If you don't call me, I'll know the Captain hasn't enough room for me.'

'Edward!' cried Chequers. 'Didn't you and I promise to stick together?'

Edward gazed up towards the point where the tall buildings of the city scraped the sky. His right nostril twitched. 'I smell a storm,' he murmured. 'By night we shall have rain.'

Then he looked tenderly at Chequers and said, 'Another night outside in the cold rain might make you sick. Please go with Jenny into Captain Tinker's house. Show him the retrieving trick I taught you. I'm sure he'll adopt you when he sees how nicely you retrieve.'

'Retrieve? What's that?' asked Jenny.

'To retrieve means to run after something and bring it back,' explained Chequers. 'This red ball I carry everywhere is my retrieving ball.'

At that moment the lunch bell sounded for the second time.

'We mustn't keep the Captain waiting,' said Jenny. 'Chequers, when we get home, you must retrieve for us.'

The three cats ran towards Captain Tinker's house. On the way Jenny asked Edward, 'Can you retrieve too?'

'No,' he answered. 'There's no trick I can do. But some day, if I find a home that has a little office in it, I should like to write.'

'Write what?' asked Jenny.

'Write about the troubles I've had,' replied Edward.

When the cats reached the house, Edward crawled into the bushes near

the open window, and Jenny led Chequers through the window, into the living room.

Captain Tinker, who was an old sailor, was sitting in his armchair, waiting for Jenny.

He must have been surprised to see her bringing home a black and white cat, with a heart-shaped face, who held a red ball in his mouth.

But the Captain was polite to cats. He let Jenny speak first.

She whispered to Chequers, 'Retrieve.'

Chequers passed his ball to Jenny. 'Hit it hard,' he said.

She batted it across the floor. He bounded after it, caught it with his teeth, returned with it and laid it at the Captain's feet.

The Captain said to Chequers, 'That was the most beautiful retrieving I've ever seen. And such a pretty ball!'

Chequers whispered to Jenny, 'Hit the ball again. I must retrieve some more to help get Edward adopted.'

But Captain Tinker picked up the ball, and looking thoughtfully at Chequers, said, 'You're hungry, and a red ball never filled an empty stomach. You must stay and eat some lunch with Jenny. After that – why, after that, you may live with us for ever, if you wish.'

'Chequers,' cried Jenny happily, 'you've been adopted. Now I'll call Edward.'

She turned towards the window. To her surprise she saw that Edward had come to the window sill without waiting to be called.

On his striped face there was a look that Jenny had never seen on any cat. It was the look of a cat gazing at something warm and beautiful which he may have to leave because he is not wanted.

'Oh!' thought Jenny. 'The Captain mustn't send Edward away; it would break his heart. I must speak to the Captain about this and try to make him understand.'

Jenny was on the point of jumping on to her master's knees to plead for Edward, when the Captain caught sight of the face at the window. And he saw Chequers glance quickly at the face. Then Chequers sat very straight and still, like someone wishing hard for something to come true.

'These two cats belong together,' murmured Captain Tinker.

Without another word he walked to the window and pulled Edward gently into the room. In that way Edward was adopted.

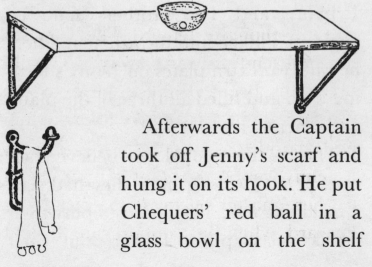

Afterwards the Captain took off Jenny's scarf and hung it on its hook. He put Chequers' red ball in a glass bowl on the shelf above the scarf.

Then the Captain said to Edward, 'You haven't a red ball and you haven't a red scarf. But you shall soon have something red, so that everyone will know you are one of us. After lunch I'll make you a red leather collar.'

'My!' thought Jenny. 'How quickly things have happened. My brothers came. They were adopted. What will happen next?'

Jenny and her brothers followed Captain Tinker into the kitchen. There he put two extra plates on Jenny's feeding tray, and filled all three of the plates with carrots and beef.

The brothers could not believe their eyes. It was so long since they had seen a meal like this. They tried to purr their thanks to Captain Tinker. But their

purrs got mixed with their food.

Each mouthful that the brothers ate put new life into their tired bodies. When lunch was over and they had washed their faces, Chequers and Edward looked like happy cats. Jenny no longer felt sorry for them.

Edward turned to her and asked politely, 'Do you think the Captain has a little office where I might do some writing?'

'Captain Tinker has gone down to his workshop in the cellar,' replied Jenny.

'I'll take you through our house. I'm sure you'll find an office somewhere.'

Jenny led Edward and Chequers up the stairs. At the top of the stairs she said proudly, 'Our house has three floors. This is the second floor, and —'

Suddenly Jenny remembered the day when she herself was adopted by Captain Tinker. The Captain, after rescuing her from trouble in the street,

had brought her into this same house and allowed her to explore it by herself, the way cats like to do.

So Jenny told her brothers, 'You may explore this second floor. I'll wait for you downstairs.'

Jenny returned to the living room and waited on the sofa. While she waited, she could hear the brothers exploring overhead, from room to room. With each step and sniff they made, she felt that Chequers and Edward were becoming more and more a part of this dear home where she had always been the only cat.

Soon Chequers came pattering down the stairs.

'Edward has found an office,' he announced to Jenny. 'It's in a cupboard, behind the Captain's rubber boots.'

Behind the Captain's rubber boots!

Jenny gulped. ... That was a place where she liked to doze on rainy days. And it was raining now.

The storm which Edward predicted had burst on the garden.

'How dark the garden looks!' exclaimed Chequers. 'It's as black as night. I guess I'll take a nap.'

Without asking Jenny's permission, he climbed into the Captain's armchair and fell asleep.

Jenny wished that Chequers had chosen another place for his nap.

'I know he's tired,' she thought crossly. 'But I'm the only cat who has ever slept in Captain Tinker's armchair.'

Then she wondered what Edward was doing: 'I bet he isn't writing at all. I bet he's snoozing.'

Jenny tiptoed up the stairs. As she passed Edward's office in the cupboard, she could hear the sound of heavy breathing mingled with delicate snores.

'Just what I thought,' she told herself. 'Well, if everyone else can take a nap, I have a right to take one too. Maybe I'll feel better after it.'

Jenny went into the Captain's bedroom, crawled into her basket and fell sound asleep. When she awakened at supper time, she felt rested and cheerful.

'From now on I'll share everything with Chequers and Edward,' she decided as she went down the stairs.

But when she entered the living room, her heart turned cold with jealousy.

Captain Tinker was sitting in his armchair. On one of his knees sat Chequers. On the other knee sat Edward wearing a new, red leather collar!

Jenny rushed towards her brothers.

'The Captain's knees belong to me,' she cried. 'Get down!'

Chequers and Edward jumped quickly to the floor.

Then the Captain picked up Jenny, stroked her cheek and said, 'Jenny, don't be jealous of your brothers. I love you just as much as ever.'

But Jenny was too upset to believe him. Before she knew what she was doing she had scratched the Captain's hand. Then, frightened by her awful deed, she fled to a safe place beneath the sofa.

Captain Tinker did not call after her or scold her. Instead, he walked quietly into the kitchen and washed the scratch. Next, he opened the door of the refrigerator. Jenny could hear him take out the supper food, warm it and fill the three plates on her tray. After that, he returned to his workshop in the cellar.

'I know why the Captain has left me,' thought Jenny. 'He wants me to make friends with my brothers. But I won't do it. Maybe I shall never speak to them again. Anyway, I'll let them eat their supper by themselves.'

She listened, but could not hear Chequers and Edward go into the kitchen. She could not hear them in the living room. Fear gripped her heart. Perhaps she'd been so horrid that her brothers had run off to find another home.

Jenny rushed into the kitchen. The brothers were not there, and they had not touched their supper.

She rushed upstairs and could not find them anywhere.

She ran downstairs and jumped on to the shelf.

Chequers' red retrieving ball was gone!

'That's it,' she moaned. 'He's taken his ball and run off with Edward. And on a night like this! Why, they may die of cold and hunger. I'll go after them, and I won't come home until I've found them.'

Jenny dashed out into the rain. She splashed across the garden, climbed over the fence and ran down the alley into South Street. There she could not tell which way to turn. The rain had washed away all traces of her brothers' paws.

She decided to turn to the right, and

ran through swirling puddles, while the rain drenched her back and filled her ears. On and on she ran, looking in every doorway. But she could not find her brothers.

At last she felt that she was running the wrong way. She stopped and asked herself, 'Where would I go on a rainy night, if I were homeless? I'd go to the fish shop, and wait in the doorway, and hope that in the morning someone would give me some fish for breakfast.'

Jenny turned back on her trail, and worked her way through the soaking rain until she reached the fish shop. There, huddled in the doorway, sat her brothers.

'Chequers! Edward!' she cried. 'I've been mean and selfish. Please forgive me and come home.'

'Jenny,' said Edward gravely, 'Chequers and I must try to find another home. We don't feel you want us in your house.'

'I do want you,' she protested.

'Do you love us?' asked Chequers.

'With all my heart,' she cried. 'To prove how much I love you, I'll let you and Edward sleep every night in my own basket in the Captain's bedroom. I'll sleep in the cellar.'

'Jenny, that proves you really love us,' declared Edward. 'We'll go home with you. But we won't take your basket. *We'll* sleep in the cellar.'

'No, I'll sleep in the cellar,' Jenny said.

'No, we will,' said the brothers.

'I will,' insisted Jenny. Then she added quickly, 'Let's not argue now, for

we should hurry home. I want to find
the Captain and beg him to forgive me
for scratching his hand.'

Jenny and her brothers ran home
through the rain. When they reached
the house they found the Captain waiting anxiously for them, with bath
towels to rub them dry.

As he rubbed Jenny's fur she tucked
her chin in the hand she had scratched,
and begged him to forgive her.

'Oh, that was just a little scratch,'
said Captain Tinker. 'You made up for
it when you ran out into the rainy night
to find your brothers.'

Then Jenny tried to tell the Captain about the sleeping basket. But he said briskly, 'Go now and eat your supper.'

So she went into the kitchen with Chequers and Edward, and ate supper.

After that, the Captain said to her, 'It's very late, and time for all good cats to be in bed. Come, see what I have built for your two brothers.'

Jenny and her brothers followed Captain Tinker up the stairs. In the room next to his bedroom stood two little bunks that he had built one above the other. Each bunk had a warm red blanket on it.

'Now no one will have to sleep in the cellar,' cried Jenny happily, while her brothers rubbed their backs against the Captain's legs and thanked him.

Chequers chose the upper bunk,

Edward climbed into the lower one, and everybody said good night.

Jenny crawled into her basket in the next room, and the Captain went downstairs to smoke his pipe. Outside, the rain beat at the window panes.

'It's good to be indoors on such a night,' thought Jenny, with a yawn.

She closed her eyes but could not go to sleep, for she kept worrying about her brothers. It would be terrible if they had run away again.

After a time Jenny crept into her

brothers' room. She found that Chequers had come into the lower bunk and cuddled in Edward's arms.

How peacefully the brothers slept! The longer Jenny watched them, the happier she felt. She also felt that someone should be thanked for all this happiness. So she went downstairs and said good night again to Captain Tinker.

HOW THE BROTHERS
JOINED THE CAT CLUB

For two nights and days it had rained
on Captain Tinker's garden, and the
cats who lived around the garden had
to stay indoors.

From time to time they pulled aside
the curtains at their windows and
stared at the Captain's house. They all
felt something strange had happened
there. Just what it was, they did not
know.

Inside the Captain's house, the little black cat, Jenny Linsky, looked out on the rainy garden and thought gloomily, 'Things might be easier if it rained for ever. Then I wouldn't have to decide what to do about the Cat Club meeting.'

Jenny's two new brothers, Chequers and Edward, came downstairs to play with her.

'Keep away from the window,' she cried quickly. 'All the other cats are looking at our house.'

'Jenny, what's the matter?' asked the younger brother, Chequers. 'Why don't you want the other cats to know you rescued Edward and me from the rain? Why don't you want your friends to know that Captain Tinker has adopted us? Don't you love us any more?'

'You're the nicest brothers anyone ever had,' replied Jenny. 'Everything I have inside this house is yours as much as mine. But after the rain stops, something special is going to happen in the garden. It's something I must decide about.'

Jenny sounded so unhappy that Edward, the older brother, said, 'Come on, Chequers. It's time for you and me to go upstairs again. I have to continue my writing, and you should practise retrieving your red ball.'

Chequers jumped on to the shelf and took his red retrieving ball from the

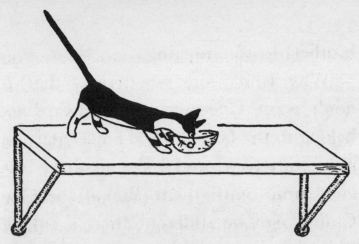

glass bowl where he kept it. He grasped
the ball between his teeth and followed
Edward up the stairs.

Jenny looked out again on the rainy
garden. The rain was stopping.

'Tonight the moon will come up,' she
thought. 'And the Cat Club will meet
beneath the maple tree. But I can't – I
really can't tell my brothers about it.
I'll steal out and go to the meeting all
alone.'

As Jenny was usually very generous,
she felt sorry about not taking her

brothers to the meeting.

'Why is it,' she wondered, 'that I don't want Chequers and Edward to belong to the Cat Club? They're part of my family now, and I should share my good times with them. But at the Cat Club I can be different than I am at home, just because my family isn't around. No one here at home – not even Captain Tinker – would ever guess the things I've done at the Club.'

Jenny had done many good deeds at the Club, and some of them had required courage. She remembered the night when she had braved a gang of wicked dogs in order to carry a flute to a sick member of the Club.

Another night Jenny had led the entire Cat Club in its parade to the park for the Annual Spring Picnic.

THE DUKE   SINBAD   ROMULUS   REMUS

JUNIOR

SOLOMON

ARABELLA &
ANTONIO

MACARONI

CONCERTINA

MADAME
BUTTERFLY   MR PRESIDENT

This chart shows the order in which the members of the Cat Club marched behind Jenny in the Picnic Parade.

The more Jenny thought about it, the more amazed she grew that she, who was so small and shy and black, had been able to do such glorious deeds. 'And I've done them, all alone, with no one to help me,' she said to herself, rather proudly.

At that moment Jenny's master, the old sea captain, Captain Tinker, came into the room. He held in his hand the bright red scarf he had knitted for Jenny long ago. One of the tassels had come loose, and he had just sewn it on.

The Captain was about to hang the scarf on its hook when he caught Jenny's eye. Suddenly she realized that what she had been thinking wasn't quite true. She hadn't done her brave deeds, all alone.

And she thought to herself, 'Without that scarf to protect me, I wouldn't have even dared to join the Cat Club. Captain Tinker helped me when he gave me the scarf, and I should help my brothers so they can get their share of fun. But it won't be easy.'

Jenny looked at Captain Tinker, and he could tell from her worried yellow eyes that she had something difficult to do.

He tied the scarf around her neck and said gently, 'Brave deeds can be done at home as well as in the world outside.'

Then he returned to his workshop in the cellar.

Jenny tucked her chin in the scarf, and the scarf gave her courage.

'I'll take my brothers with me to the Cat Club,' she decided. 'Even if it spoils a little of my fun, I'll do it.'

Now that she'd made up her mind, Jenny felt much better.

She went upstairs to find her brothers.

Jenny found Chequers practising his retrieving in the hall. Retrieving his little red ball was a trick Edward had

taught him while they were wandering
homeless through the wide, wide world,
before they came to live with Jenny.

Chequers had chosen one corner of
the hall for his home base. He would
stand on the home base, bat the ball
down the hall with his paw, chase the
ball, pick it up with his teeth and carry
it back to the base. Chasing the ball
and bringing it back was called 'retrieving'.

Jenny loved to watch her black and
white brother retrieve, but right now
she had other things to do.

'Chequers,' she said, 'I'm sorry I was
cross with you downstairs. I was busy

making up my mind about our Cat Club. Most all the cats who live near here belong to it. We'll meet tonight, and you and Edward must go with me to the meeting. I'll ask if you may join the Club.'

'Is it hard to join?' asked Chequers.

'Quite hard,' admitted Jenny. 'No one is allowed to become a member unless he can do a special trick. You'll get in all right because of your retrieving trick.'

'And Edward's trick can be his writing,' said Chequers.

'Yes,' agreed Jenny, 'writing will be Edward's special trick.'

But suddenly an awful thought occurred to her: what if Edward couldn't write?

It was true he'd found an office for

himself in a corner of the cupboard, behind Captain Tinker's rubber boots. Edward had spent many hours in his new office. But maybe he had only been sleeping there. So far he hadn't shown Jenny anything he'd written.

'Chequers,' she said, 'I'm afraid we'd better speak to Edward.'

The two cats poked their noses into the closet where their older brother (a gentle cat with handsome tiger stripes) was lying comfortably behind the Captain's boots.

'Edward,' said Jenny, 'excuse us for bothering you. I'm sure you're very busy. But there's something you should know.'

Edward looked up from the floor.

'It's about our Cat Club,' continued Jenny. 'We meet whenever there's a moon, and there will be a moon tonight.'

Edward's soft eyes brightened.

'We have a President, a Secretary and eleven regular members,' explained Jenny. 'Our motto is

Loyalty, Fidelity, Truth and Dues. I hope you and Chequers will be allowed to join the Club.'

'Thank you,' said Edward. 'It sounds very exciting.'

'But you must be able to do a special trick,' continued Jenny. 'Chequers, of course, can retrieve. When I joined the Club, Captain Tinker made me some ice skates and I skated. If it were winter now, instead of spring, I'd lend my skates to you.'

'Skating is your trick, not mine,' said Edward. 'Mine must be my writing.'

Jenny said, 'Would you have a piece of writing you could read to us, just to see if it's the kind of thing the Cat Club likes?'

'I haven't had time to do any real writing,' admitted Edward. 'But I've been thinking about a poem I'd like to write some day. It would begin like this:

'I'd love to be a butterfly
Flying high – flying high.'

Edward stopped and looked up hopefully. 'What do you think?' he asked.

Jenny thought to herself, 'I think it's awful. But I can't tell him so. I'd hurt his feelings.'

'Please tell me the truth,' he begged.

Poor Jenny said nothing. The truth was too hard for her to tell.

But the word 'truth' kept running through her mind. Where had she heard the word before? Loyalty, Fidelity, *Truth* and Dues. It was the third word in the Cat Club motto.

So she decided to tell Edward the

truth. And she realized it would be better for him to learn it now, when it might help him. She would try to tell it nicely, so he wouldn't feel too hurt.

'Edward,' she said bravely, 'the Cat Club is tough. Most of the members are older than you, and they might think your poem is babyish. You should give them something scary. Something that will make their fur stand up. Something that will make their whiskers twitch – and *shiver*.'

'Shiver their whiskers,' murmured Edward. 'H'm. I know the poem to write.'

A faraway look crept into Edward's face. He hunched his shoulders, and the claws of his right paw scratched the floor. Edward was writing!

Jenny went downstairs with

Chequers and they jumped on to the sofa.

'Jenny,' said Chequers, 'you must be tired after all you've done. Let's take naps and have a rest before the meeting.'

They snuggled together, and while they slept, Jenny had a terrible dream about Edward's not being allowed to join the Cat Club. She woke up with a start and found the sun was shining brightly.

Chequers woke, too, and went upstairs. He came down immediately and said, 'Edward is still writing. He'll see us at supper.'

When Edward heard Captain Tinker

rattling the supper dishes, he came downstairs.

'Did you write a scary poem?' asked Jenny.

'Shiver my whiskers! I did,' he declared. 'But it would be bad luck for me to tell you what it is before the Club meeting.'

After supper the three cats got ready for the meeting. With licks of their pink tongues, they washed their furry coats and smoothed their whiskers.

When the moon shone on the garden, things began to happen. Bushes stirred, shadows moved across the grass. Jenny stood watching at the window, while her brothers sat near her on the floor.

'I'll keep you a secret till the meeting gets started,' she said. 'Rough cats like Sinbad and The Duke can think up lots

of trouble if they have too much time
for thinking. Those two are coming
now.'

Other cats were also rushing to the
meeting. Jenny named them: the twins,
Romulus and Remus; Solomon, the
wizencd wisc cat who accompanied the
President's young nephew, Junior; the
sweethearts, Arabella and Antonio; the
fancy dancer, Macaroni; and the fluffy
Madame Butterfly, who could play
sweet music on a nose flute.

'There goes our Secretary,
Concertina,' whispered Jenny. 'She's
climbing up the maple tree, where she
scratches records of our meetings.

Everybody's there except Mr President. Oh! He's coming now. Let's start. Chequers, have you your retrieving ball? And don't forget you're to wait with Edward in the bushes till I call you.'

Jenny gave one last anxious look at Edward, who was nervously muttering his poem. Then she jumped into the garden. Her brothers followed, and while they crawled into the bushes, Jenny sped to the meeting. She arrived just as it opened.

'Does anyone have any special business to discuss?' asked Mr President.

Jenny waved a small black paw.

He said, 'Jenny, name your business.'

Her heart thumped as she began: 'Mr President, I have two wonderful new brothers. Their names are Chequers and Edward.'

All eyes stared at Jenny. So that was what had been happening in her house. New brothers. Two of them!

'Please, Mr President,' she continued. 'May my brothers join this noble Cat Club? They're waiting in the bushes.'

'Bring forth the brothers,' ordered Mr President.

Jenny ran to the bushes and returned with her brothers. The members gave Chequers a friendly nod, because his red retrieving ball looked so exciting. But Edward seemed like such a gentlemanly cat that Sinbad and The Duke began to giggle.

'Silence,' commanded Mr President. 'Chequers and Edward shall be

discussed in alphabetical order. C. comes before E. Will C. step forward?'

Chequers picked up his red ball and went before Mr President. Mr President asked him his name and where he lived. Chequers answered in a clear, sweet voice.

Next Mr President asked him, 'Can you do anything?'

'I can retrieve,' answered Chequers.

Chequers rolled his ball to Jenny, who batted it with her paw across the moonlit grass. He dashed after it, brought it back and laid it before Mr President.

No one had ever seen such fine retrieving. The members raised their paws and voted Chequers into the Club.

As Chequers returned to his seat, Jenny made a silent prayer: 'Please may Edward pass his test, too.'

Then Edward was called before Mr President, who asked him the usual questions: name, address and what he could do.

To this last question Edward answered, 'I can write.'

'Please read a writing,' said Mr President.

Edward said, 'I shall recite a poem.'

'A poem!' shouted The Duke. 'Who wants to hear a sissy poem?'

This rudeness startled Edward. His voice left him. Standing alone in the ring, he looked so helpless that Jenny was frightened.

After a long time Edward stammered in a little, tiny voice, 'I am a ghost'.

A ghost! Though he had said it softly, Jenny and the other members caught the scary word. Their fur stood up. Their whiskers twitched – and *shivered!* Sinbad and The Duke called out to

Edward, 'Louder, please! And start again!'

This time, in a stronger voice, Edward said, 'A Poem by Edward Brandywine.'

A POEM

BY
EDWARD
BRANDYWINE

I am a ghost.
Though I don't want to boast,
I'm the ghost of a pirate cat —
That's that.
In times gone by,
Oh me, oh my!
In another life
I carried a knife
With a pointed tip
At my snarling lip
And sailed on a ship
With a sword at my hip
As a pirate cat —
That's that.

With a hearty *meow*
I'd leap from the prow
To another ship's deck
And there I'd wreck
All cats on board
With my trusty sword
And the knife from my lip
And the tigerish skip
Of a pirate cat —
That's that.

As time flew by
My crimes piled high.
But what did I care
As I sailed here and there
Till, alas! I was caught.
What a battle I fought!
But they whisked me apart
And pickled my heart,
And my life on a ship
With a knife at my lip
As a pirate cat
Fell flat.

Now in olden times, when this tale
  took place,
A wicked cat was granted a grace:
Nine lives had he —
Nine chances to be
A good, respectable cat.

So here at last,
With my crimes long past,
I stand expectant-ly.
More tales I could tell
And they'd all sound well.
A rhyming cat – *that's me.*

Edward bowed graciously to indicate
that his poem was finished. Modestly he
tried to return to his seat. But the other

cats were pushing towards him, cheering the great writer, Edward Brandywine. Immediately they voted him into the Club.

'Speech, Edward! Speech!' cried Sinbad, whose whiskers were still shivering with excitement from the pirate poem.

The Duke and the other members took up the cry: 'Speech, Edward! Speech!'

Jenny gazed proudly at her brother Edward as he said, 'I wish to thank the Cat Club for the great honour it has paid me.'

'How beautifully he speaks and writes,' thought Jenny.

Then she could hear Edward say, 'I also wish to thank my little sister, Jenny Linsky. If Jenny hadn't helped me, I could never have written my poem.'

'Me?' wondered Jenny. 'What did *I* do?'

And Sinbad said to Edward, 'Tell us, what did Jenny do?'

Edward smiled.

'Jenny helped me find the proper kind of poem to write,' he answered. 'She told me I should make your whiskers shiver.'

Someone with a heavy paw pushed Jenny through the crowd. She stood happily between her brothers while the Cat Club gave three cheers for Jenny Linsky.